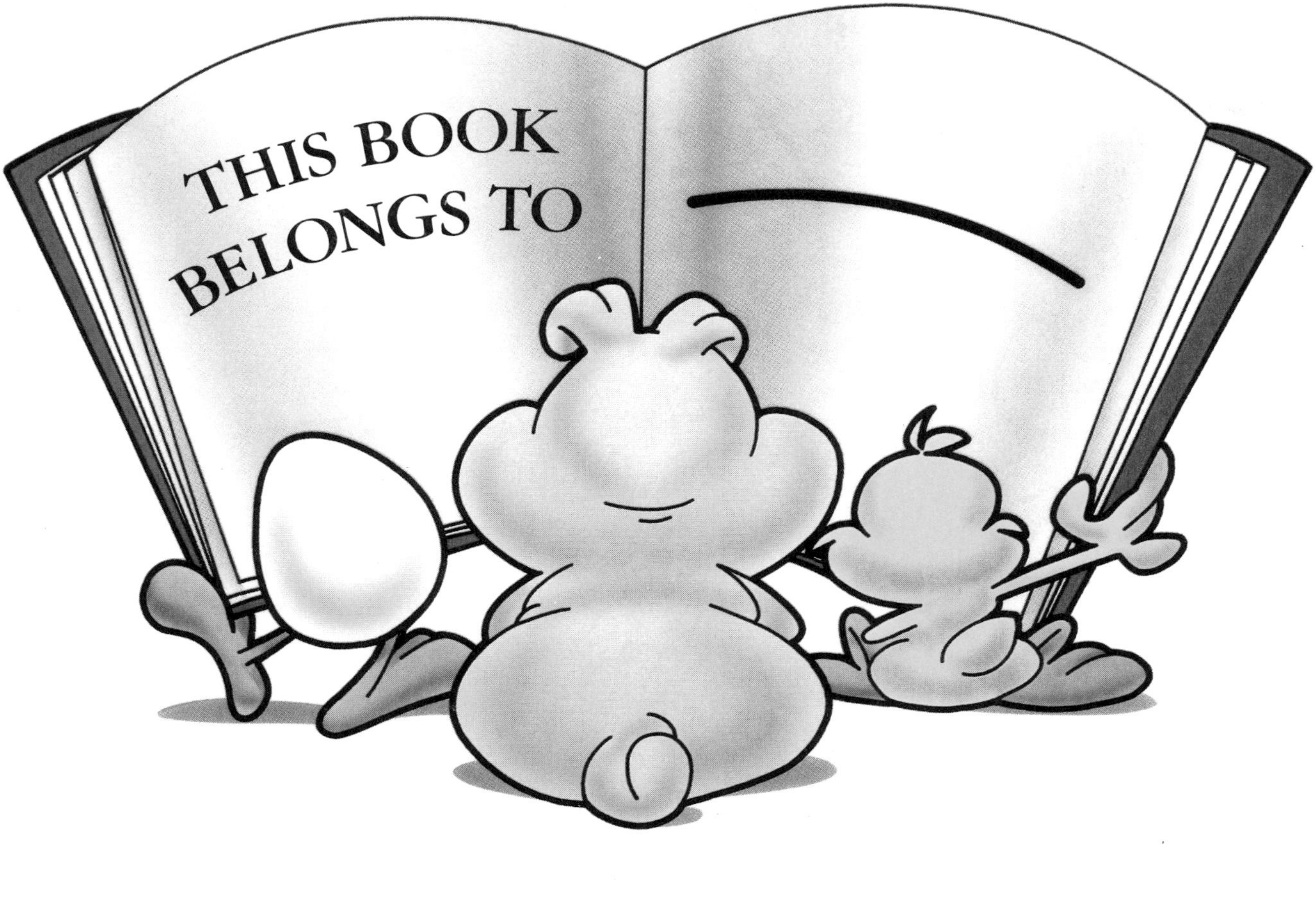
THIS BOOK
BELONGS TO

BANTAM BOOKS
NEW YORK · TORONTO · LONDON · SYDNEY · AUCKLAND

Jim Davis

U.S. ACRES

BOOKER MEETS THE EASTER BUNNY

from the creator of GARFIELD®

Written By Jim Kraft
Designed By Brett Koth
Illustrated By Brett Koth,
Dwight Ferris, and Thomas Howard

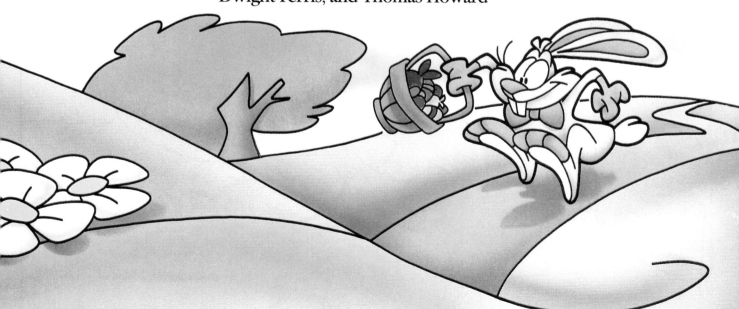

It was the night before Easter, and chickens were stirring in the barn.

"Come back here, you Easter Bunny!" cried Booker to his brother, Sheldon. "I want your candy!"

"You'll never catch me!" replied Sheldon, hopping out of reach.

"Ooof!" grunted Orson. "I wish you boys would settle down. I've never seen you so excited about Easter."

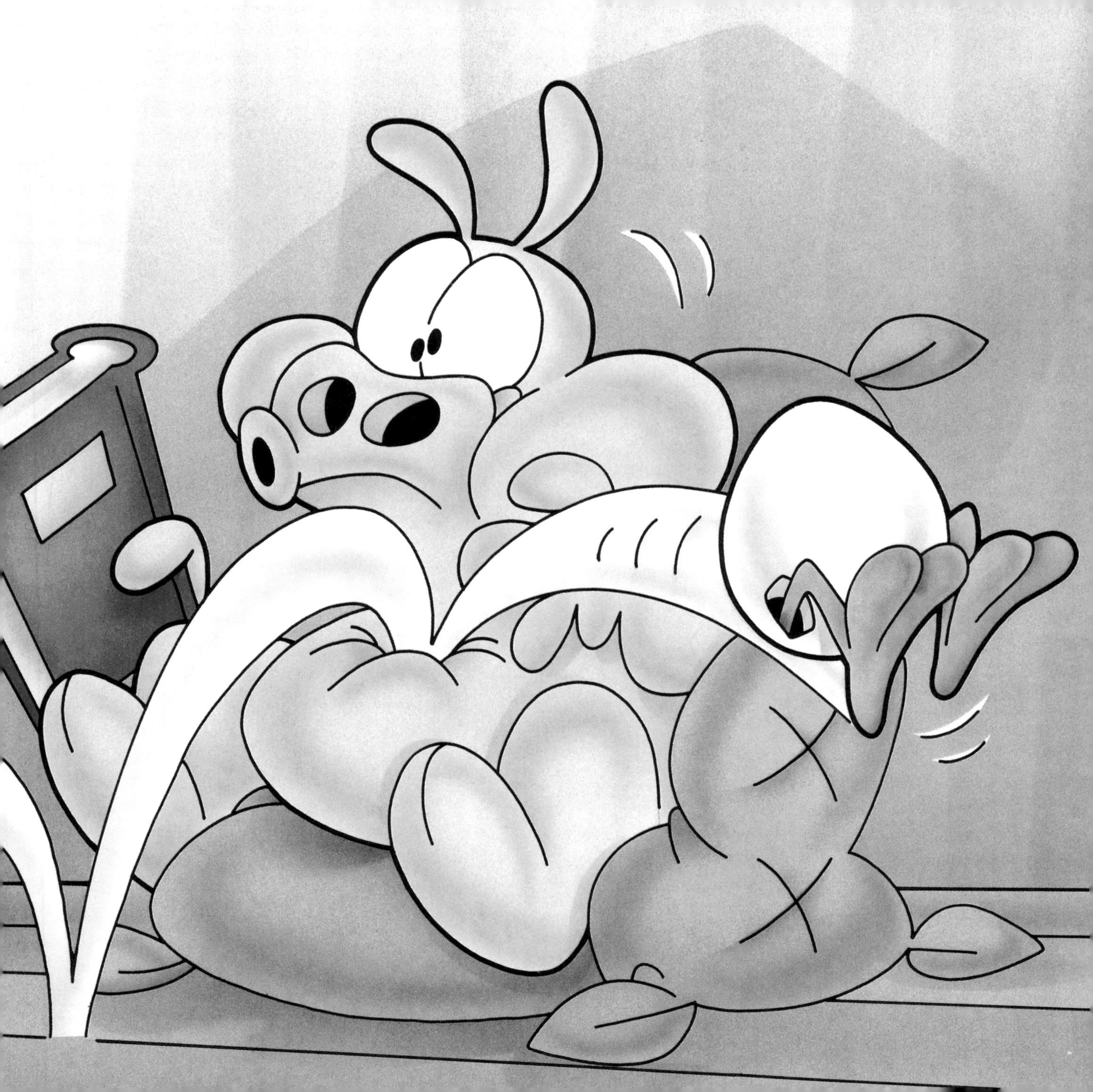

"Of course we're excited!" said Sheldon. "Tomorrow morning these baskets will be packed with Easter treats! I can't wait to gobble those jelly beans!"

"I *love* Easter candy!" Booker said. "I never get enough. I wish the Easter Bunny would leave *all* of his candy just for me."

"Then the rest of us wouldn't have any," Orson reminded him.

Booker laughed. "So what? I'd be too stuffed to care!"

Lying in bed, Booker pictured his Easter basket overflowing with chocolate bunnies and marshmallow chicks and jelly beans and all sorts of delicious treats.

"I want more," Booker murmured to himself. "I want it all."

Suddenly, he sat up. "And I think I know how to get it!"

Booker slipped out of bed and crept outside to the garden. There he collected the biggest carrots he could find. He set the carrots on a plate beneath a big tree.

Next Booker made a sign and hung it on the tree. The sign read:

FREE CARROTS!
ALL YOU CAN EAT!
EASTER BUNNIES WELCOME!

"That should get his attention," said Booker.

Finally Booker fetched a large butterfly net from the toolshed. Then he hid behind the tree and waited.

Soon the Easter Bunny came hopping by. He stopped to read the sign.

"Free carrots!" he exclaimed. "I think I'm going to like this job!" The Easter Bunny reached for a carrot. Booker raised the net.

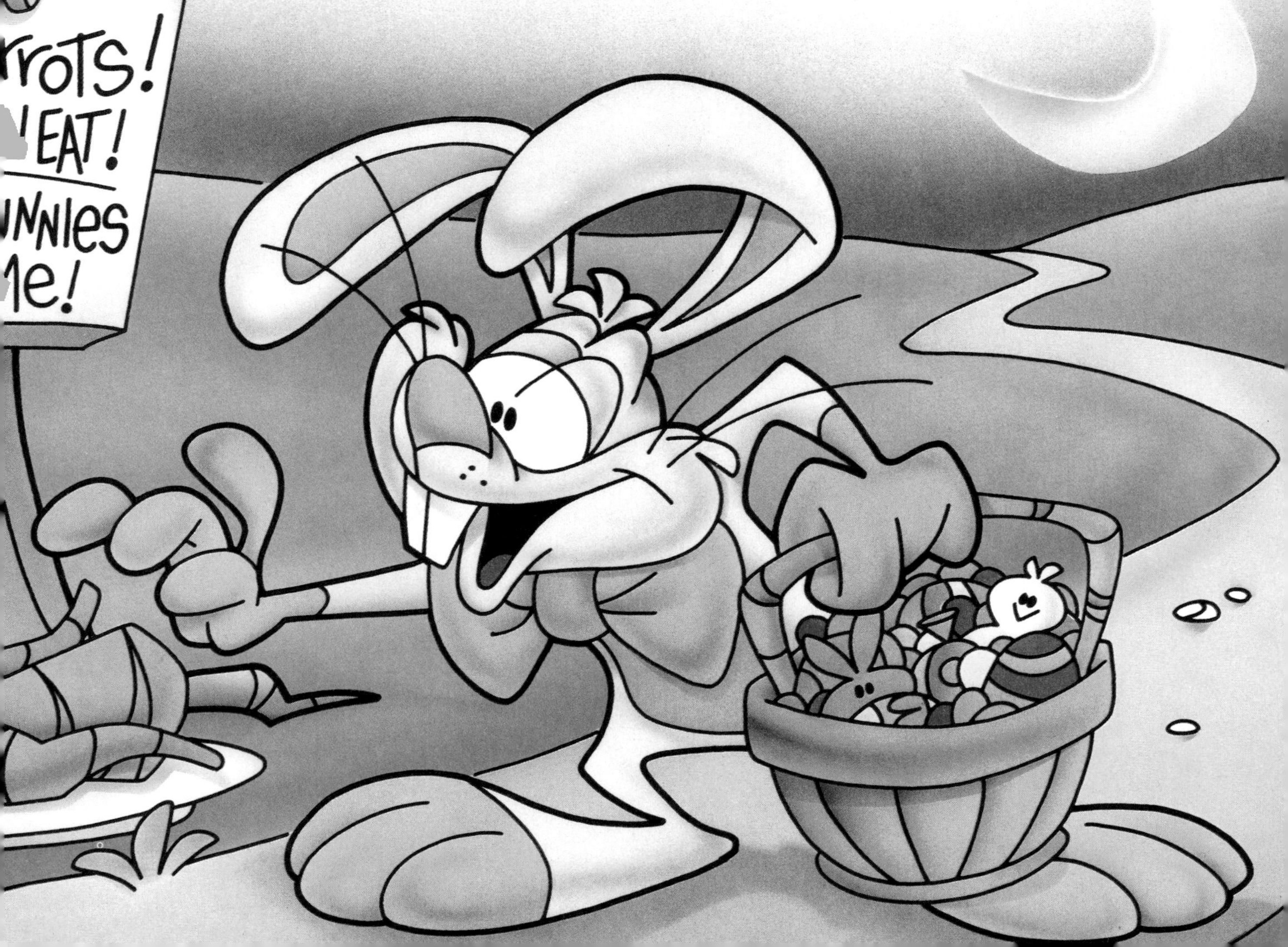
EAT!

"Gotcha!" cried Booker.

"WHOA!" cried the Easter Bunny.

"I did it! I captured the Easter Bunny!" crowed Booker. "And now it's candy time!"

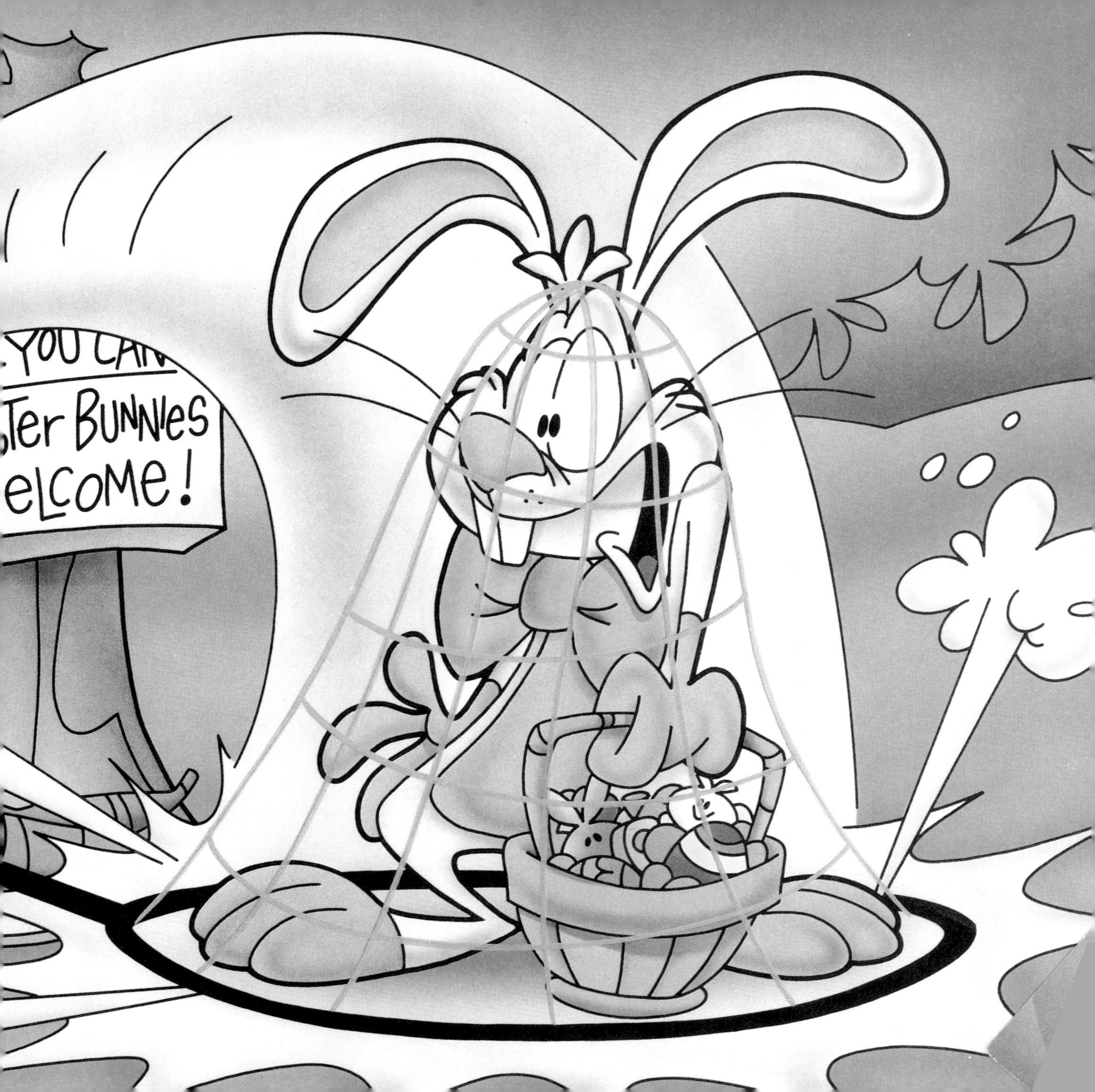
YOU CAN
STER BUNNIES
ELCOME!

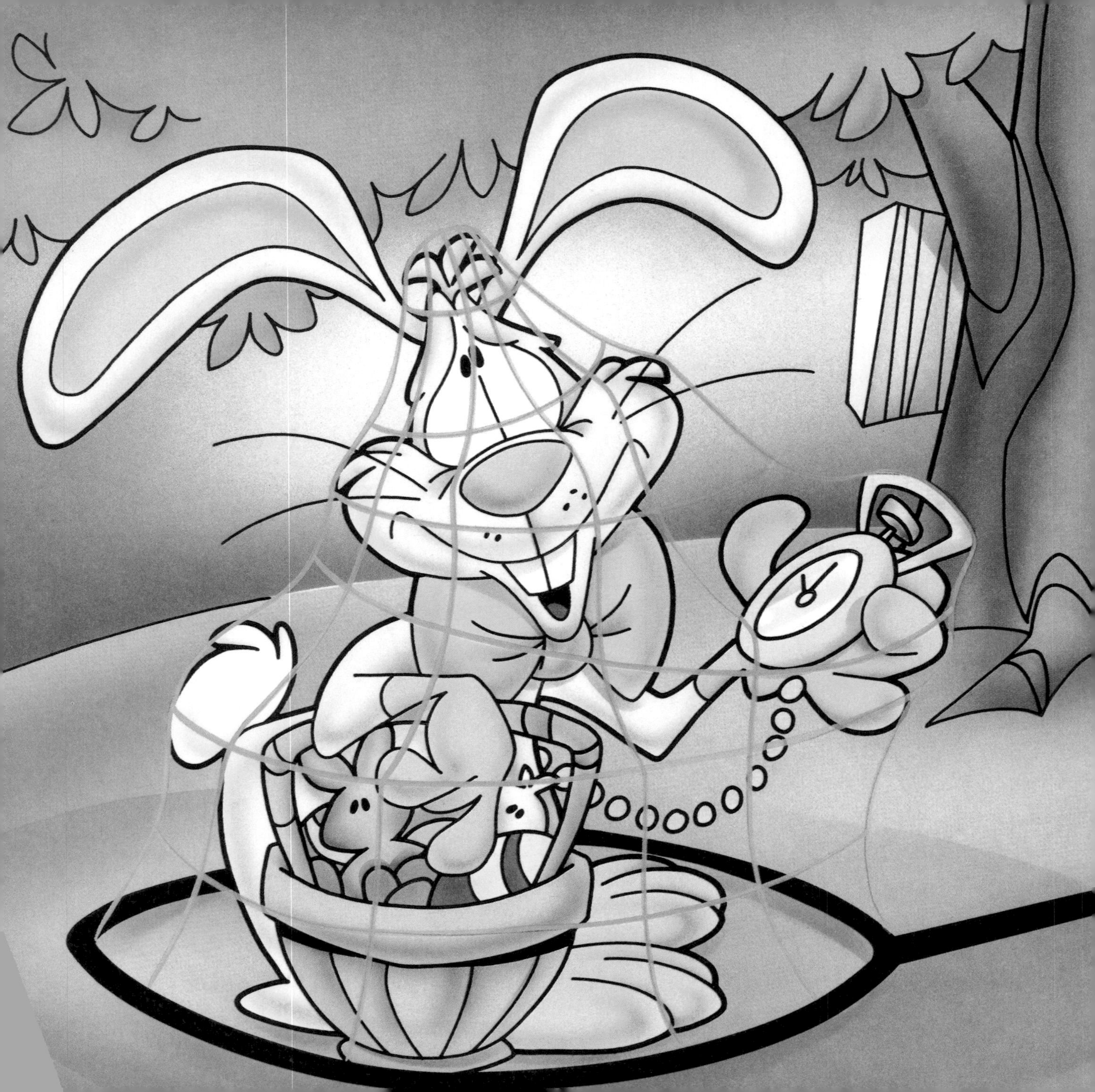

The Easter Bunny gave Booker a puzzled look.

"Oh my," said the bunny. "Is this supposed to happen? He never told me anything about this."

"Who never told you?"

"The old Easter Bunny. He's retired, you know. Lives on a carrot ranch in Florida. I'm his replacement. This is my first Easter on the job."

"How's it going?" asked Booker.

The bunny groaned. "I'm already running late. And now this!"

"You need help," said Booker. "I know . . . why not give your candy to me. I'll deliver it for you."

"Oh, I couldn't!" replied the bunny. "It's against the rules. I'd lose my job."

"Then just give me all the candy for U.S.Acres. I can deliver *that* for you, right?"

The bunny looked doubtful. "I'm supposed to deliver the treats myself."

"You're already late," Booker reminded him. "Besides, the *old* Easter Bunny let me do this all the time."

"He did?" The bunny wiggled his ears thoughtfully. "Well, in that case . . ."

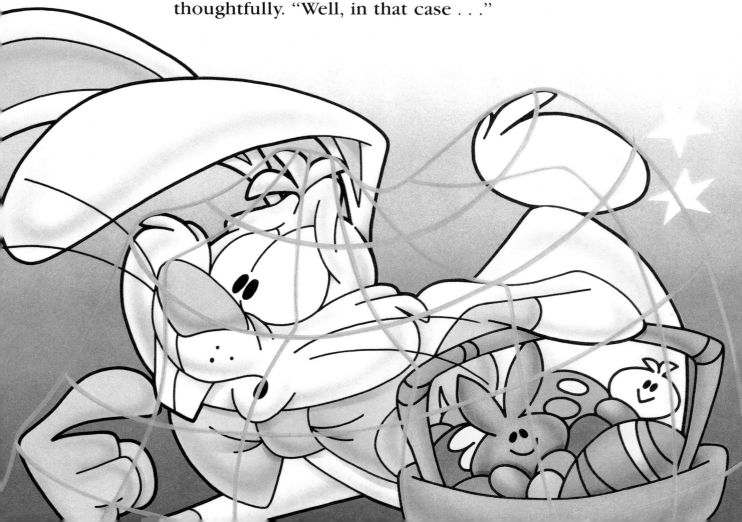

Booker freed the Easter Bunny, who hopped off to complete his duties, leaving Booker with a large heap of Easter treats.

"Look at all these jelly beans and cream eggs and chocolate bunnies!" exclaimed Booker. "And they're all mine!"

Booker ate and ate until his tummy started to ache. And still there was a mountain of candy left!

Should I give some to the other animals? he wondered. Nah, they probably don't like candy that much anyway.

It was nearly dawn. Booker quickly tossed
the rest of the candy into a wheelbarrow and hid
the wheelbarrow in the toolshed. Then he crept
back to bed and was soon dreaming of his
candy treasure.

That morning Booker was awakened by the sound of Sheldon's crying.

"Booker! Booker! It's terrible!" sobbed Sheldon. "The Easter Bunny never came! We didn't get *any* treats!"

The whole gang was very upset.

"There must be an explanation," said Orson. "The Easter Bunny wouldn't forget us."

"Maybe he was kidnapped by chocolate-loving space aliens," suggested Wade.

"I'm going to write the Easter Bunny a nasty letter!" shouted Roy.

"I'll never trust a bunny again!" vowed Lanolin.

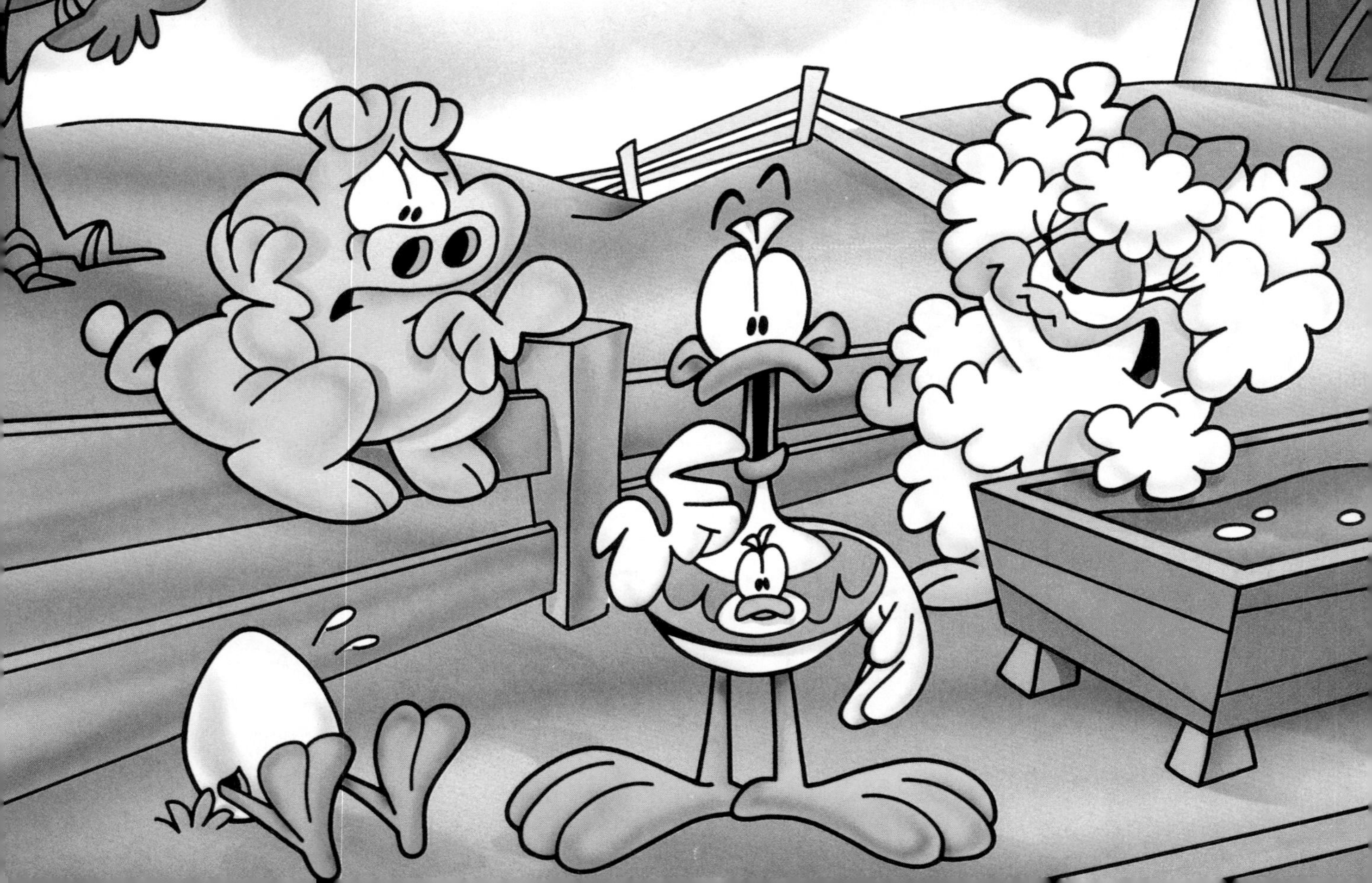

Booker began to feel guilty. "Maybe the Easter Bunny made an honest mistake," he said.

"Fat chance!" countered Roy. "He's probably keeping our candy for himself."

While the others fumed, Booker sneaked off to the toolshed.

"I feel awful," he said. "I've ruined Easter for everyone, including *me*. How can I enjoy these treats when my friends are so unhappy?"

"We could still fix that," said a voice.

"You came back!" said Booker.

"I had to," said the bunny. "I heard all the complaining."

Booker hung his head. "It's all my fault. But what can we do?"

"Are all the other animals in the barnyard?" asked the bunny.

"Yes."

"Then we've got to act fast!"

Scampering from building to building, Booker and the Easter Bunny filled the empty baskets with Easter treats.

"Will we have enough?" whispered Booker. "I ate a lot last night."

"Don't worry," said the bunny. "There might
even be enough to fill *your* basket."

When the unhappy animals discovered their
Easter baskets full of treats, they were overjoyed!
"This is more like it!" said Roy.
"Jelly beans!" cried Sheldon. "My favorite!"
"The Easter Bunny left a note," said Orson. "It
says, 'Sorry I was late. I took a wrong turn at
Muncie. Happy Easter!'"

Booker and the bunny watched the celebration.
"Sharing those treats with your friends certainly
made them happy," observed the Easter Bunny.
"It makes me feel good, too," said Booker.

The Easter Bunny yawned. "Time for me to go," he said.

"Thanks for not telling them I took their candy," said Booker.

"Don't mention it. But don't ever try to fool the Easter Bunny again!"

"I won't," promised Booker. "Not for all the candy in the world!"